nickelodeon
TEENAGE MUTANT NINJA
TURTLES

SHOWDOWN WITH
SHREDDER

Adapted by Matthew J. Gilbert

Based on the teleplays
"Showdown, Part 1" and "Showdown, Part 2"
by Joshua Sternin and Jeffrey Ventimilia

RANDOM HOUSE 🏠 NEW YORK

Published in the United States by Random House Children's Books,
a division of Random House, Inc., 1745 Broadway, New York, NY 10019,
and in Canada by Random House of Canada Limited, Toronto.
Random House and the colophon are registered trademarks of
Random House, Inc. Nickelodeon, Teenage Mutant Ninja Turtles,
and all related titles, logos, and characters are trademarks of
Viacom International Inc. and Viacom Overseas Holdings C.V.
Based on characters created by Peter Laird and Kevin Eastman.

randomhouse.com/kids

ISBN 978-0-307-98225-4

Printed in the United States of America
10 9 8 7 6 5 4 3

DIMENSION X

In the farthest reaches of the galaxy, past every starfield and through every wormhole, there is a cosmic realm unlike any other in the universe . . . Dimension X! Here, the icy vacuum of space is powerless against the smoldering meteors. Here, clusters of comets ignite the cosmos like an intergalactic fireworks display. Here, there are no actual stars, and hence, no planets capable of supporting life.

Except for one.

But it isn't a real planet. Real planets aren't made of titanium armor and grinding gears. A living world wouldn't have all-terrain tank wheels and rocket boosters. This is a planet-sized war machine with rivers of glowing mutagen pulsing through it. This is an extra-dimensional space station capable of destroying solar systems. This is . . . the *TECHNODROME*.

Inside the control room, Kraang-droids— robotic exoskeletons that housed the blobby, brain-like Kraang, a race of alien villains—mapped the *Technodrome*'s flight plan to a secret location. At the very moment they were setting the coordinates, a holographic video display flickered to life. The droids stopped what they were doing, as this could mean only one thing—

"A message from Kraang's glorious leader," a droid announced, "Kraang Prime!"

The Kraang respectfully saluted their commander: "Kraaaaang! Kraaaaang! Kraaaaang! Kraaaaang!"

Suddenly, a hologram appeared like a window floating in the middle of the control room.

Meanwhile, on Earth, businessmen hailed cabs and tourists posed for photos, all completely unaware that just underneath their feet a team of mutant ninjas was springing into action.

Deep down in the sewers, where the Teenage Mutant Ninja Turtles lived, Donatello and April O'Neil—the Turtles' only human ally—rushed into Donnie's high-tech lab. At that very moment, it seemed like every piece of technology he owned was going out of control!

"Holy Toledo!" Donnie panicked.

The network of computers he had programmed to intercept Kraang transmissions was on the fritz. And why wouldn't it be? Donnie knew the gear he'd gotten from the local electronics store was no match for alien tech that was light-years ahead of anything on the market! The dual-core processors could barely keep up with the volume of Kraang symbols scrolling on the screen. And the Kraang Sphere—a strange device the Turtles had recovered a few weeks ago—was emitting a piercingly loud sound.

Over the noise, Donnie managed to hear April yell, "What's with the alarm?"

"The Kraang communication orb's going haywire," he explained, trying to get things back under control. "Which means those little brain-blobs are up to something *big*!"

April stared in horror at the Kraang symbols as they continued to download. What more could these slimy creatures want? They had already kidnapped her father and nearly ruined her life. "Can you decode this stuff?" she asked.

"Guess we're about to find out," Donnie said, typing a long string of commands into his computer. "Translating . . . now."

Donnie and April called the other Turtles— Leonardo, Raphael, and Michelangelo—into the lab. Leonardo, the leader of the group, was in no mood for entertaining Donnie's techno-babble if it meant missing the season finale of his favorite TV show, *Space Heroes. Captain Ryan was about to sacrifice himself to save his crew,* Leo thought, *and I'm missing it for what? What could be so important?*

"April and I have been sifting through all this Kraang chatter and, well, listen to this," Donnie said. He keyed in a code and brought the Kraang translations up on a screen.

Suddenly, the robotic voice of a Kraang-droid boomed over the computer speakers. "The final phase of the plan known as Kraang's Invasion shall commence in the unit of time that is six hours. The *Technodrome* shall arrive from Dimension X through the portal."

Leo, Raph, and Mikey glanced at one another, dumbfounded.

"Are you sure this is the translated version?" Mikey asked.

Donnie shot him an exasperated look. He began to translate for the group. "They said, in six hours, something called the *Technodrome* is coming through the portal. This is the final phase of the Kraang invasion!"

Leo was confused. "Wait, but I thought April was the key to the Kraang plot," he said. "And they don't have her."

It was true. A few weeks earlier, the Turtles had uncovered a Kraang storage device that was similar to a hard drive. It contained two very important things: encrypted instructions to terraform the earth . . . and images of April! It was clear she was meant to be part of their evil plan, but the reasons why were still a mystery. At least to the Turtles.

"Guys, if that *Technodrome* comes through the portal . . ." Donnie hesitated. "Well, it sounds like the end of the world."

"So what do we do?" Raph asked Leo.

"We've got to find a way to shut that portal down," Leo answered. "It's up to us."

"To save the world?" Mikey asked.

"Leonardo is right," a voice said from the shadows.

The Turtles all looked up to see Splinter, their wise ninja master. He looked even more serious than usual. After all, it wasn't every day that a parent sent his children out into the world to stop an alien invasion. Controlling his emotions, Splinter faced the Turtles and readied his words of wisdom.

"When you first went up to the surface," he began, "I feared you were not ready. But I have come to realize that not only were you ready to become heroes . . . it was your destiny."

The Turtles hung on his every word.

"And if the fate of the world must rest in somebody's hands," he told them, "I am grateful it is yours."

And with that, they respectfully bowed to Master Splinter, knowing what time it was—time to shell out some justice!

Splinter pulled Leo aside. "With the world

at stake, the only thing of importance is that you complete your mission," he privately instructed.

Leo understood. "Yes, Sensei."

Splinter's eyes locked with Leo's. "No matter what you have to sacrifice . . . or who."

CHAPTER 2

"Good luck, guys!" April said, watching the Turtles gear up for their big mission. Without thinking, she gave Donnie an innocent hug—which made him absolutely euphoric. He'd been crushing on her since the day they'd met, and now she was actually hugging him! He had stars in his eyes—until he saw April kiss Mikey on the cheek.

Filled with jealousy, Donnie started in on Mikey. "How did you—?" he stammered. "Why did she—?"

Mikey paused, and then confidently said, "Some dudes got it, and some dudes don't."

"Gentlemen," Leo said to his brothers, in a voice that would make the Space Heroes proud, "let's go save the world." In formation, the Turtles boarded their battle cruiser, the *Shellraiser,* ready to kick some Kraang butt!

Nearby, April and Splinter stood together and watched the Turtles head out into the unknown.

In spite of the odds stacked against them, Splinter saw that his sons were ready to charge into battle. It was a truly heroic moment.

Until the *Shellraiser*'s door suddenly opened to let Mikey out. He waddled past April and Splinter, disappearing into the bathroom. They looked at each other, wondering what was going on.

Moments later, they heard the toilet flush.

Leo emerged from the *Shellraiser*'s doorway. "Okay, does anybody else have to go?"

Mikey quickly returned to the van, slamming the door shut. The *Shellraiser* roared to life and headed down the sewer tunnels into battle.

Splinter and April were completely alone.

Something had been troubling April all night, but she wasn't sure how to bring it up to Splinter. Sure, she was his friend, but she was also his student—Splinter had taken her on months ago as a *kunoichi,* a student of *ninjutsu*—and asking her teacher anything personal could be seen as disrespectful. But April had to say something.

"Um, Sensei, why aren't you going with them?" she asked.

Splinter was caught completely off guard. "Why do you ask?"

"Well, the Turtles are out there risking their lives," April said. "Don't you think they could use your help?"

"I am their teacher," he told her. "My role is to prepare them for the challenges they face."

That's not good enough,

April decided. She needed to know why he wasn't prepared to fight alongside his sons. "But, Sensei, you said yourself that this time the fate of the world is—"

"Damare!" he shouted, which is Japanese for *Silence!* He glowered at her. "I do not have to explain myself to a child!"

Enraged, Splinter stormed off. And not a moment too soon, as he could no longer hide his shame. The master's usual cold, stoic expression was now one of embarrassment. April's words hadn't hurt him because they were disrespectful— but because they were true.

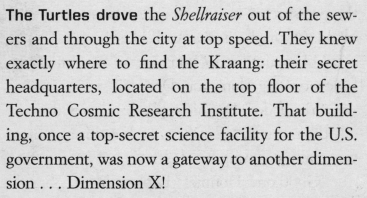

CHAPTER 3

The Turtles drove the *Shellraiser* out of the sewers and through the city at top speed. They knew exactly where to find the Kraang: their secret headquarters, located on the top floor of the Techno Cosmic Research Institute. That building, once a top-secret science facility for the U.S. government, was now a gateway to another dimension . . . Dimension X!

"All right, guys, we're going to keep it simple," Leo told his brothers. He gestured to a strange-looking device that Donnie had stowed inside the *Shellraiser*. "We go to T.C.R.I., and we use the Micro-fission Omni-disintegrator, which Donnie calculates is powerful enough to destroy the portal with a single shot."

"Then why didn't we use it last time?" Mikey asked.

"Because we didn't have it last time," Donnie explained.

They'd only been in the *Shellraiser* a few minutes, but Mikey and Donnie had already had enough of each other. Maybe it was the pressure of having to save the entire world. Or maybe it was April's kiss.

Mikey muttered, "You have an answer for everything, don't you, Donnie?"

"Yes, I do," Donnie replied. He was usually the rational, scientific type, but this argument was really steaming his shell!

"Good one, Donnie!" Raph smirked. "Speaking of 'good one,' you sure this plan will work, Leo?" he asked.

A hush suddenly fell over the van. Leo kept his eyes on the road. "It has to work."

CHAPTER 4

Back at the Turtles' lair, April was nervously pacing around the room when a feeling of dread washed over her: she wasn't alone! A tall, slender man was right behind her.

"Hey, April, where is everybody?"

April breathed a sigh of relief. It was only her dad, Kirby O'Neil, who—just a week ago—had been rescued by the Turtles from a secret Kraang detention center.

"The Kraang are making their move," she explained. "The Turtles are on their way to T.C.R.I."

April watched her father carefully as he reacted to this news. She was happy to be reunited with him, but lately she'd noticed something different about him. Something strange. Clearly, his experience with the Kraang had traumatized him.

"T.C.R.I.?" Kirby said, weary. "Oh no . . ."

"What's wrong?" April asked as her father began to twitch uncontrollably.

"The Kraang are aware that the Turtles are coming for them," Kirby insisted.

"How do you know?" April grabbed her T-Phone and started dialing the Turtles, when Kirby snatched it away from her.

"Don't!" he yelled.

After a long pause, Kirby composed himself and tried to put on a calm face for his daughter. "The Kraang have cracked the T-Phone's encryption. We've got to warn the Turtles in person." He looked at April meaningfully. "I'm your father, April. You have to trust me."

Those words really got to April. How could she say no to her dad when he was only trying to help her friends? So she let Kirby lead her out of the lair, toward the surface.

Just then, Splinter emerged from the shadows.

"April, where are you going?" he demanded.

April stood up to her sensei. "The Turtles are in trouble. I've got to go warn them."

"But you know it's dangerous for you to be on the surface," Splinter reminded her.

April forced herself to stay strong. "Well, some of us can't just sit around and do nothing."

And with that, April caught up to her father, ascending to the wide-open city above their heads.

"Dad, what are you doing?" April asked as she noticed they were getting farther and farther off course. "This isn't the way to T.C.R.I."

"We have to go this way so we won't be spotted," he assured her. "Hurry!"

But April didn't want to go any farther. Not until he started acting like her father again. "What are you talking about?" she asked him. "Dad, what's going on?"

Kirby put his hands on his daughter's shoulders. And now that April could feel how much he was trembling, she could tell he was struggling with some intense, indescribable urge.

"I'm sorry, April," he said sadly.

She was confused. But then she watched his eyes glaze over until they were as vacant as a robot's.

"For what?" April asked.

Threatening figures in black suits appeared and quickly surrounded her. It was a Foot Clan ambush!

"Hey there, princess," a voice called from the crowd. A beautiful teenage *kunoichi* stepped forward with the confidence of a highly trained assassin. It was Shredder's daughter, Karai!

"Miss me?" she asked April.

"Yeah, actually," April said through clenched teeth.

Their previous encounter had been neck-and-neck ninja battle. The two *kunoichi*s had exchanged kicks and power-punches in the street, fighting for their lives. April had finally managed to gain the upper hand by sweep-kicking Karai down onto the subway tracks.

"Last time I saw you," April started, "I forgot to give you this!"

Thwaack! April knocked Karai to the pavement with a swift kick.

The Foot Clan quickly overpowered April, preventing her from unleashing any more blows.

Karai eyed her adversary with grudging admiration as she got back up on her feet.

Splinter has taught you well, she thought.

Karai signaled for the Mousers—Baxter Stockman's miniature mechanical minions— to gather around Kirby.

"You've performed admirably," she snarled at him. "Now take the message to Splinter."

It was clear to April now: her father had been hypnotized into some sort of trance by Shredder's army. On autopilot, he began marching back toward the sewers with the Mousers in tow.

"Dad, what are you doing? Dad?!" April pleaded. But it was no use. The man she called Dad was merely a puppet under the enemy's control.

"You brainwashed him!" April yelled.

"I know," Karai acknowledged. "Pretty cool, right?"

With just a nod, Karai commanded her Foot Soldiers to drag April away, screaming into the darkness.

CHAPTER

5

T.C.R.I. was under extremely tight security that night. Several Kraang-droids patrolled the lobby. They were each heavily armed with energy blasters and were guarding their secret base with eerie, mechanical precision. If this place was ground zero for the Kraang invasion, then everything had to run smoothly.

Craaaash! The *Shellraiser* smashed through the lobby windows in a hail of shattered glass. Before its tires hit the floor, the Kraang-droids opened fire on the Turtles' van. Glowing energy bolts shot from their blasters, burning holes in the side of the vehicle.

Convinced the Turtles were Swiss cheese by

now, the Kraang-droids ceased fire. A thick fog filled the lobby from their still-smoking blasters. A hazy silence descended over the room.

Then the *Shellraiser*'s roof hatch opened, and a Turtle-like figure started to emerge. But the Kraang-droids' scanners weren't recognizing it as one of the Ninja Turtles. Whatever this was, it seemed unstoppable. Mechanical.

It was Metalhead—the Turtles' robo-sidekick!

"Boo-ya-ka-sha," Metalhead announced in his robotic voice before deploying each of his high-tech weapons and firing all at once like an un-beatable battle machine.

At the moment the T.C.R.I. lobby was explod-ing into smithereens, a fleet of small aircraft soared through the starry sky overhead. The Teenage Mutant Ninja Turtles were flying safely above the battle on homemade hang gliders.

Pleased that his decoy plan had worked, Donatello continued to control Metalhead with a small device he held in the palm of his hand.

Raph smiled. "Nice work, Donnie!" Coming from the toughest Turtle with the most attitude, that was a huge compliment.

"Do you know what it's time for?" Mikey announced. "The world's first-ever midair high three!"

The Turtles used the wind to steer their gliders in formation and executed a flawless four-

Turtle high three. So far tonight, they were on a roll.

"This is awesome!" Mikey yelled, as psyched as ever. "Turtles were born to fly!"

"All right, guys, let's do this," Leo commanded. They zoomed through the air, banking as one toward the T.C.R.I. rooftop.

As soon as the Turtles touched down, they silently stowed their gliders and waited for Leo's orders. Giving them the all clear, he signaled Raph to block the security camera so they could remain unseen.

Evading security was one of Raph's many talents, and luckily, he had just the right tool to cover the camera lens: a pigeon.

Inside the building, in a secret Kraang surveillance room, a lone Kraang-droid watched the wall of video monitors. It didn't notice the screen showing the pigeon. Its attention was focused on the live security feed of Metalhead's ongoing armored assault in the lobby.

Back up on the rooftop, everything was much calmer. The two Kraang-droids who were standing guard had no idea the Turtles were sneaking up behind them. "It is quiet," one Kraang-droid announced. "Precisely the correct amount of quiet."

Just then, Mikey popped up to distract them: "Wah-booga-booga-wooh!" Before the Kraang-droids could react, Donnie leaped at them with his *bo* staff and knocked them off the roof with one swift move.

The droids plummeted several stories to the sidewalk below, muttering their last words in free fall:

"This is going to leave that which is known as a mark."

"Affirmative."

CHAPTER 6

Back at the Turtles' *dojo*, Splinter attempted to meditate, but it was no use—his soul was restless. Memories of his argument with April kept breaking his concentration.

The last words she'd spoken to him echoed in his mind: "The Turtles are out there risking their lives. Don't you think they could use your help?"

Ashamed of his own inaction, Splinter dug even deeper, trying to focus instead on the silence. But after a few moments, more of April's words came flooding back: "Well, some of us can't just sit around and do nothing."

Just then, Splinter's heightened ninja senses recognized a change in the room. There was an intruder in his *dojo*. With a slight flick of his wrist, Splinter grabbed his cane and rolled effortlessly into a striking stance, swinging his weapon inches away from—

April's father, Kirby.

The hypnotic trance Kirby was under was so powerful, he had no idea how close he'd come to getting hit in the face! All he could do was continue mindlessly staring down the end of the cane at Splinter.

"Where is April?" Splinter asked.

"Master Shredder wanted you to have this message," Kirby recited.

A horrified look of confusion came over Splinter's face. "Master . . . Shredder?!"

As he struggled to understand Kirby's words, Splinter heard another disturbing sound: the pitter-patter of dozens of little robotic feet. The Mousers emerged from behind Kirby, flashing their steel fangs.

They delivered the message, projecting a flurry of lights that flashed and then morphed into the shape of a mysterious stranger. It was a hologram of Splinter's worst nightmare . . . SHREDDER.

"So, Hamato Yoshi, you thought you could hide from me forever," the hologram said. "But now I have April O'Neil, and if you value her life, you will come and face me like a man. And we will finish what we started all those years ago."

And with that, the hologram dissolved into the shadows.

Hamato Yoshi. In a different lifetime, it had been the name of a man who lost everything to Shredder. A man who had fled his native Japan in search of a new life. A man who had lost his humanity one fateful day when a mysterious canister of ooze mutated him into a giant rat. Hamato Yoshi was the true name of Master Splinter.

Remembering all the pain Shredder had caused him, Splinter closed his eyes in misery. When he opened them again, he looked determined, and ready for a fight.

CHAPTER 7

Despite the surveillance cameras everywhere, the Turtles managed to sneak into T.C.R.I. unseen with the Micro-fission Omni-disintegrator. The strange device may have looked like a simple hand cannon, but it had enough energy inside to destroy the portal with just one shot. Or so the Turtles hoped!

They leaped up to a hanging walkway high above the floor. From this vantage point, they could see a massive generator down below that was hissing and popping with electric bolts. With each charge, the shapes formed a gateway that grew bigger and bigger!

"It's the portal!" Donnie realized. Confidently, he began calculating the best place to blast it, when he noticed a giant figure standing guard.

"It's Traag," Raph said. "I forgot about him."

Raph recognized the chiseled features of Traag—a rock monster from Dimension X that stood over twenty feet tall! He was loyal to the Kraang, and his cosmic DNA made him nearly indestructible.

"Don't worry," Donnie calmly said. "We'll be gone before that rock monster even knows we're here."

Leo activated the Micro-fission Omni-disintegrator. This was it. The fate of the world rested on this one shot. "Okay, guys, this all ends in three . . . two . . . one—"

Leo held his breath as he squeezed the trigger. A neon energy beam came blasting out of the weapon—

And then dissolved in midair with a tiny *pfffft*.

The Turtles were shocked.

"The portal must be protected by an invisible shield," Donnie said.

Leo gave his brother a look. "There's a force field?! Why didn't you tell me?"

"Well, because I wanted us to fail," Donnie sarcastically replied. "Obviously, I didn't know!"

Suddenly, energy bolts came whizzing by their heads. They had been seen! An onslaught of Kraang-droids attacked, blasters blazing.

Raph yelled, "Anyone got a Plan B?"

Seconds later, the Turtles saw something come hurtling toward them—Traag!

CHAPTER 8

Shredder's lair was hidden in plain sight. To the untrained eye, it looked like an abandoned church in a dangerous neighborhood. Every floor had stained-glass windows adorned with dust and caked-on bird poop. Faded graffiti covered the walls in splashes of red and purple. The breeze swirled trash at the bottom of the front steps.

Stationed on the ground were four Foot Soldiers. Their instructions were simple: attack and capture anyone who came down this street. But they hadn't seen anyone stupid enough to come through this part of town in years. For the past few hours, they had been staring at nothing, waiting for any sign of someone. . . .

An old drifter rounded the corner, shuffling toward them. He was frail and wore a hood that covered his face.

The Foot Soldiers relaxed.

They had no idea who they were dealing with.

Inside the building, behind closed doors, Shredder's mutant henchmen, Dogpound and Fishface, anxiously awaited their master's sworn enemy. They'd heard stories about Hamato Yoshi, but tonight, they were certain they'd get to meet him face to face.

"So how good is this so-called ninja master anyway?" Fishface asked with a snarl.

"He's as skilled as Master Shredder," Dog-pound explained. "But he doesn't have the stomach to finish the fight."

Just then, they both heard a commotion outside the lair.

"What was that?" Fishface asked.

"He's here!" Dogpound growled.

The two mutants threw open the doors and drew their weapons. On the steps before them, the Foot Soldiers were lying in a pile, beaten unconscious.

Dogpound and Fishface looked at each other. They knew Splinter had to be close by.

Fishface could feel his blood boiling. His gills flared out. "Come on out, you sniveling—"

THWACK!

Before Fishface could react, Splinter dropped down from the ceiling behind them, attacking with lightning-fast ninja precision. In one complex move, he dispatched both mutants, knocking them out cold before they even hit the floor.

CHAPTER 9

While Splinter was across town delivering a surprise attack, the Turtles were getting one—from Traag! The two-ton alien rock monster was in their path, barreling toward them. With every step he took, the hanging walkway buckled under his immense weight. The Turtles were trapped.

Traag vaulted, propelling himself into the air. He prepared to bring his full weight down on the Turtles. But before he could squash them, Leo lifted the Micro-fission Omni-disintegrator and squeezed the trigger.

He fired the white-hot energy beam, blasting Traag apart in a fiery explosion of gravel and space dust that settled on the floor below. Leo couldn't believe it had actually worked! Thinking they had beaten Traag, the Turtles breathed a sigh of relief.

But then the Kraang-droids began blasting energy bolts at them. And as if that weren't bad enough, tiny bits and pieces of Traag inexplicably started coming back together. It was like some invisible magnet was helping him re-form without a scratch on him.

With the situation spiraling out of control, Leo cornered Donnie. "Donnie! How's that Plan B coming?"

"I'm thinking!" Donnie shouted.

The fully re-formed Traag was back in action! He hurdled up and over the railing and landed back on the walkway with a loud *CRASH!*

"Think faster!" Leo commanded.

Seeing no other option, Leo opened fire on Traag again. And in a brilliant flash of light, Traag exploded once again into a hail of flaming pieces.

There was no time to celebrate. Before the smoke cleared, Traag's molecules began to re-form. Leo knew they couldn't keep this up forever.

Donnie was starting to feel the pressure. He didn't have a solution. There was no exit strategy for something like this. He needed to rely on what he knew best. Whipping out his trusty laptop, he turned to Leo. "I can probably hack into the Kraang system if you give me enough time!"

"Great! Do that!" Leo said, trying to manage the situation before it got any worse.

As Donnie went off searching for a computer port, the remaining Turtles put their shells together and tried their best to cover him. But with an oncoming army of Kraang-droids, and a freshly resurrected Traag, they knew this battle was about to get ugly.

CHAPTER 10

Splinter found April inside Shredder's main chamber. She was locked in rusted shackles. Opening his special ninja lock-picking kit, Splinter approached her quietly.

"April, it is me," he whispered. "Do not make a sound. I will have you out in a moment."

Splinter reached for her wrists and gasped. His hand passed right through April's as if she were a ghost. She wasn't really there. He had been deceived by a hologram!

From the shadows behind him came a laugh he had not heard in decades: a deep gurgle that would send chills up anyone's spine.

Splinter spun around to look his archnemesis,

Shredder, in the eye. This was no hologram. The spikes before him were real, and the dangerous foe beneath the armor was flesh and blood staring back at him. It was a nightmare come true.

"Hamato Yoshi, I am so glad you accepted my invitation," Shredder said maliciously.

"What have you done with April?" Splinter demanded.

Shredder's voice boomed from inside his metal mask. "Now that you are here, Miss O'Neil is no longer of any use to me." He then added, "I gave her to my new friends . . . the Kraang."

Splinter knew that with April in their possession, the Kraang were one step closer to achieving their plans for world domination. He was stunned. "You fool! Do you have any idea what you've done?!"

"Yes," Shredder retorted. "I took your family away, and now I've lured you here so I can put an end to you once and for all!"

Splinter heard the crash of the chamber doors slamming shut, followed by the click of a lock.

These two ninja masters, who had been at war their entire lives, were now trapped in a concrete cage with no chance of escape.

Prepared to literally face his fears, Splinter removed his hood, revealing his rodent face to Shredder for the very first time. The Hamato Yoshi that Shredder once knew—a man, a husband, a father—was now a mutant in sewer-soaked rags.

"A rat? A rat?" Shredder laughed wickedly. "I see you are as hideous as those Turtles that surround you. How fitting. You're a rat who has been caught in my trap."

Splinter could feel his anger rising. He knew the only way to finish this fight was the way of ancient *ninjutsu*—where fist meets foot, good meets evil, and only one warrior is left standing. Through his teeth, Splinter muttered, "Look closely at this face, Shredder, for it is the last thing you'll ever see!"

Back at T.C.R.I., the Turtles were getting nervous. The Micro-fission Omni-disintegrator was taking longer and longer to fully charge. This meant Traag had even more time to re-form each time. Leo knew, when dealing with an enraged rock monster of this size, an extra second could mean the difference between life and death.

"Come on! Come on!" Leo pleaded, waiting for the weapon's power bar to refill.

The last molecule in place, a re-formed Traag angrily thundered toward the Turtles. His gargantuan stony fists were raised high, ready for squashing. Leo's eyes grew wide. The device was still charging, and Traag was gaining on him with every step. For a moment, it looked like they were about to be crushed into Turtle dust.

Just then, the Micro-fission Omni-disintegrator let out a small *beep*. Leo once again squeezed the trigger, and a glowing energy pulse shattered Traag into a million tiny pieces that went flying through the air. Leo let out a tiny sigh of relief. For a swordsman who rarely handled firearms, he was getting pretty good at this. He looked down at the weapon's ever-dimming battery light. "This thing's running out of juice!" he called out.

"And, guys . . . look!" Mikey said suddenly. Beyond the packs of Kraang-droids, the Turtles could see the portal to Dimension X opening up.

Its array of cosmic lights lit up the force field with an eerie, electric glow.

"Whatever's coming through the portal is gonna be here soon!" Leo said, knowing they were running out of time.

Just behind him at a nearby computer console, Donnie attempted to hack into the Kraang's complex system. Meanwhile, Raph and Mikey were dodging blaster fire from the Kraang.

Exhausted, Raph impatiently yelled, "When's that force field coming down, Donnie?"

"I'm working on it!" Donnie shouted, his fingers rapidly punching in codes. Deciphering alien computer systems was extremely difficult, but trying to do it under fire, lasers whizzing by constantly, made it nearly impossible.

Another barrage of energy bolts came raining down on the Turtles as Traag took form again. Leo looked down at the Micro-fission Omni-disintegrator's battery screen—it was moving so slowly, it didn't seem to be recharging at all. Leo looked back up just as the rock monster's eyes reopened and it roared back to life. Traag was furious. With stone fists swinging, he thrashed through the room on a path of destruction. Leo saw one of Traag's boulder-sized fists about to come down on his head.

"Not good!" Leo said, rolling away to safety right before—*CRASH!*—Traag smashed a crater into the floor right where Leo would have been standing.

Suddenly, the weapon beeped on. Leo popped back up onto his feet and disintegrated Traag with an energy beam at point-blank range. Traag was nothing but particles!

Donnie found some good news on his computer. "I think I got it!" he shouted.

The force field dimmed, flickering into nothing. Donnie smiled. With the craziest line of code, and under the harshest battle conditions, he had prevailed! This would go down in hacker history. "Yes!" Donnie celebrated. "All hail me!"

But they were too late. Something massive had already started to come through the portal.

"Uh-oh, guys!" Donnie said, seeing the structure take shape as it materialized into their dimension. They had never seen anything quite like it. It was round like a planet, and so big that it cast a wide shadow from deep space over every square inch of T.C.R.I. Even the Kraang-droids stopped their attack to stare in awe at its majesty.

It was a mechanical monument. A destroyer of worlds. An airship sent from Dimension X. It was the *Technodrome*!

CHAPTER 12

Mikey stared wide-eyed at the airship coming through the portal. "Holy giant floating shippy-ship!" he screamed. "Leo! Do the zippy-zappy thing! Now!"

Quickly, Leo lifted the Micro-fission Omni-disintegrator and put the portal generator right in its cross hairs. The weird-looking weapon had served him well tonight. Hopefully it had enough juice to finish the job!

"Say good night, Kraang!" Leo said confidently.

Thinking he was about to end the Kraang invasion with one shot, Leo happily squeezed the trigger. But nothing happened! Only a sputter of sparks came out before the battery died for good. The weapon was toast.

"What the heck happened?" Donnie asked.

"I think the battery died!" Leo answered.

"And we'll be joining it unless someone thinks of something," Raph added.

"What's Plan C, Leo?" Donnie asked in a panicked voice.

With a crazy look in his eye, Leo asked, "Donnie, what would happen if we ruptured the power cell?"

"The whole place would go up, with you in it!" Donnie warned. He looked at his brother's serious face. "Whoa, Leo. You're not thinking what I think you're thinking!"

But he was. And there was no way anyone was going to talk him out of it. "Everybody get out of here!" Leo said sternly.

"He's thinking it!" Donnie said, backing away.

Donnie, Raph, and Mikey took off toward the roof, heading for safety. They all knew what was about to happen.

Leo drew his trusty *katana* blades and visualized his route to the power cell. He could see the crowds of Kraang-droids in his way, but he wasn't going to let them stop him. He summoned his courage. It was now or never. So he flew into action!

Leo evaded the first wave of Kraang-droids with a series of flips and somersaults. As he broke through untouched, a second wave of armed droids stormed him, and Leo unleashed a fury of *katana* strikes.

He sliced and diced his way through the Kraang, leaving a mass of blown circuits and broken robot parts behind him. He sprinted toward the power cell. He was getting closer.

But so was the *Technodrome.*

Just as the mechanical monstrosity was about to fully materialize through the portal, Leo went airborne. With one final push, he front-flipped, plunging his *katanas* into the power cell with a fierce downward thrust! A nest of sparks ignited. A devastating energy wave was about to blow this building, and everything in it, sky-high.

Leo spun around. He needed to get out of there. He ran for the roof, when—*KABOOOOM!*—the power cell erupted in an off-the-charts explosion. In an instant, glowing flames consumed everything in a white-hot cloud. The shock wave blew Leo off the side of the T.C.R.I. building before it burst into smithereens.

Leo was in midair and falling fast.

CHAPTER
13

As every floor of T.C.R.I. exploded into rubble behind him, Leo flailed through the air. The busy streets of the city grew closer and closer. There was nothing to break his fall, no chance of surviving a drop like this.

But then a small aircraft streaked across the sky and caught him. It was Raphael, piloting his homemade hang glider!

"Gotcha!" he said. Once Leo was safely secured, Raph shouted, "Woo-hoo! In your face, gravity!"

A look of relief came over Leo. There, hang gliding alongside them, were Donnie and Mikey. All of the Turtles had survived and succeeded!

T.C.R.I. was history. The portal was no more. Earth was safe. Mission accomplished!

"Thanks, Raph!" Leo said finally.

"Anytime, buddy!" Raph said.

As the smoke from the explosion cleared, streaks of pink-orange light illuminated the sky. None of the Turtles could believe what he was seeing. After a life of living underground in the darkest sewers, and patrolling the city at night only, they were about to experience their very first sunrise.

Not as freaks, not as strangers, but as heroes!

The Turtles looked at one another, beaming over their victory.

"I can't believe it! We saved the world!" Donnie said enthusiastically.

"Yeah." Mikey smiled. "That wasn't so hard, was it?"

But as he spoke, an ominous shadow covered his face. Sensing something was very wrong, he looked at his brothers in midair, and then to the streets below. Darkness was covering everything.

They all looked to the sky in horror. Something colossal was eclipsing the sun.

It was the *Technodrome*!

The Kraang airship from Dimension X had somehow made it through the portal before the blast.

In that moment, the truth of the situation dawned on the Turtles. They hadn't stopped the invasion at all. In fact, the planet was in more danger now than it had been at the start of their mission.

Mikey immediately regretted his earlier comment. He was stunned, disappointed, and afraid. "I gotta stop saying stuff like that," he mumbled.

CHAPTER 14

All across the streets of New York City, millions of people came to a standstill. Traffic cops stood with their mouths open. Street cleaners froze midsweep. Buses and cabs paused in gridlock, their drivers unaware that the traffic light had turned green. Life as they knew it had suddenly stopped. People everywhere stood staring at the *Technodrome* as it loomed over them.

High above the sea of frightened faces,

the Turtles found themselves hang gliding directly into the airship's line of fire.

"I think I speak for all of us when I say . . . *AAAAH!*" Mikey shouted.

"What the heck is that thing?" Raph asked.

"It's the end of the world!" Leo answered.

"Actually, it's just the end of humanity's reign as the planet's dominant life form, " Donnie said. "Like when the dinosaurs—"

"Now? Really?!" Leo yelled, cutting Donnie's lecture off. "You're gonna do this *now*?"

"Well, excuse me, but it's how I deal with stress!" Donnie yelled back.

"Well, maybe it doesn't have weapons!" Raph said uncertainly. "Does it look like it has weapons?"

Just as the Turtles started to study the *Technodrome,* a huge three-pronged laser cannon emerged from the ship's main weapons hatch. It made a mechanical whirring noise and then blasted an energy bolt directly at them!

"I think it has weapons!" Leo screamed. "Evasive maneuvers!"

"Right!" Mikey agreed.

Using a strong gust to push forward, the Turtles soared through the air, banking their gliders on a diagonal away from the *Technodrome*. They acrobatically rolled through the crosswinds, flying over the vulnerable city.

CHAPTER 15

Seeing Shredder up close was like staring at fear itself. But Splinter knew that after months of being tormented by nightmares about this very moment, he had the courage to look his archenemy in the eye. After all, he reminded himself, under the armor and beneath the razor-sharp mask, Shredder was just a man.

A man he had known many years ago by another name.

"Oroku Saki," Splinter said, naming Shredder aloud. "You were once my friend. I thought of you as my brother."

The memories of Splinter's former life as Hamato Yoshi came flooding back to him: his village in Japan, the sliding wood-and-paper doors of his modest house, and the people living there who made it a home.

"Fifteen years ago, I was a different man," Splinter said. "I had everything I could want. A loving wife—"

He remembered the face of a beautiful woman. Those soft, welcoming eyes he would wake up to each morning. That smile that could warm his heart and make him fall in love each time he saw her. Her name was Tang Shen.

"—and a beautiful daughter," he went on, remembering the newborn girl he had once held proudly in his arms. *Let's name her . . . Miwa,* he could hear himself telling his wife.

Then Splinter's memories took a dark turn. "And you, my loyal friend. Jealousy consumed you," he recalled, seeing the silhouette of an unwanted visitor in his mind. From behind the paper panels of the sliding doors, the shadowy figure watched his unsuspecting family. The menacing shape suddenly morphed into the outline of Shredder!

"You sought that which was mine," Splinter said angrily, snapping back into reality. It was time to make Shredder pay for what he'd done. "You took everything I loved. Everything! And still you hunt me down!"

As Splinter charged at Shredder, that fateful night flashed before his eyes: the sight of his attacker, the face of his baby girl, the sound of his wife screaming through the darkness, the flames . . .

By the time he'd heard Tang Shen's shriek echo across the village, it was already too late. Their house was ablaze and she was trapped inside. He finally fought off Oroku Saki, but did he have enough time to save her? With just steps left to go, he watched his house crumble, then burn up into black smoke. That was the instant he lost everything. Overcome with grief, Hamato Yoshi didn't see Oroku Saki sneak off into the shadows carrying a mysterious object. He only saw the flames before him rise higher. He saw the smoldering embers dissolve into nothing. He saw life as he knew it vanish. He fell to his knees, screaming out into the night—

The scream jarred Splinter back to the moment. He knew this fight was his destiny. And he knew the only way to fulfill it would be to take Shredder down.

"So I fight you now," Splinter announced to Shredder, stealthily moving into striking distance. "To end this."

CHAPTER 16

The Turtles continued to hang glide through the clouds over the tallest skyscrapers in the city. But even at top speed, the airship was closing in fast.

Mikey decided to try an evasive move all his own. He scraped past Donnie's glider and banked abruptly.

"Whoops!" Mikey yelled out, but it was too late. His glider collided with Donnie's, and both Turtles started falling!

Leo, who was still hitching a ride with Raph on his glider, tried to steer after them.

"Donnie! Mikey!"

They crashed to the street.

Leo looked down. After what seemed like an

eternity, he saw movement. Donnie and Mikey were A-okay! Leo breathed a sigh of relief. But that feeling was very short-lived.

The *Technodrome* unloaded energy blast after energy blast at them.

"What now?" asked Raph as he steered the glider from side to side.

Leo knew there was only one answer: if they wanted to survive the *Technodrome*'s terrible firepower, they'd have to spin their glider around and fly underneath it. But the moment their glider turned—

BLAM! The *Technodrome* blew them out of the sky!

They rocketed toward the cement. Leo had already avoided one giant fall this mission, but he wasn't going to avoid this one.

Leo and Raph hit the pavement hard.

Donnie and Mikey ran to the hang glider wreckage.

"Are you guys all right?" Donnie asked.

Leo opened his eyes and nodded at Donnie

and Mikey. Then he looked over at Raph.

Wincing, Raph managed to sit up. "I've been better," he answered. He noticed that his brothers were staring into the distance. As Raph followed their gaze, he found himself looking at a scene that could have come straight from a disaster movie: the *Technodrome* was wreaking havoc across the city. With nothing standing in its way, citizens scrambled in horror, looking for any kind of shelter from the extra-dimensional war machine. It was mass hysteria!

"What do we do?" Donnie wondered out loud.

"We need to talk to Splinter," Leo told them. "Come on."

The Turtles lifted a manhole cover and began their long trek back down to the lair, far from the *Technodrome*'s all-seeing eye.

CHAPTER 17

When the Turtles arrived back at their lair, they expected to see April and get some guidance from Master Splinter. But their home was empty. Their living room was ransacked. Something was very wrong.

"Hello? Sensei?" Leo called out. But no one answered.

"April?" Donnie called. There was nothing but silence.

Then Raph pushed ahead of everyone in a full-blown state of alarm. There was only one name on his mind. "Spike!" He yelled out.

Just then, across the room, a tiny reptilian head popped up. It was Raph's pet turtle, Spike, and he was perfectly safe under a toppled table.

"Thank goodness," Raph said as he rushed over to hug his pint-sized pal. "Don't scare me like that, buddy."

Mikey wandered into the *dojo* behind everyone else. "Anyone in here?" he asked, just before—WHOOSH!—someone tried to take him out with a swing of a *hanbo* staff. It was April's dad, Kirby!

"Whoa, dude, chill!" Mikey shouted before pulling off a swift back handspring to dodge another *hanbo* strike.

The other Turtles quickly wrestled Kirby to the ground.

"What the heck is going on?" Raph asked.

Something caught Donnie's eye, and he stared at Kirby. At the base of his skull was the glint of a micro-sized square implanted beneath his skin.

"Guys, check this out," Donnie said, pointing out the curious device.

They all noticed the tiny chip, then looked at each other, confused.

It didn't take long for Donnie to extract the

computer chip from Kirby's head. He showed off the weird piece of nanotechnology to the other Turtles.

Totally stumped, Leo asked, "So . . . what is it?"

"I think it's a mind-control device," Donnie explained.

That got Raph excited. "Really?" he interjected, swiping the chip and chasing Mikey around with it.

"No! Stop it! Stop it!" Mikey yelled, doing his best to keep Raph at bay.

"Raph!" yelled Leo.

Suddenly, they all heard a low groan coming from the couch in the living room. The brotherly bickering would have to wait: Kirby was slowly regaining consciousness.

"Mr. O'Neil," Donnie said softly. "Are you okay?"

Remembering only fragments of last night's double-cross, Kirby hung his head in shame. "I've done something terrible," he confessed.

"It wasn't your fault, Mr. O'Neil," Donnie

reassured him. "Just tell us what happened."

Kirby sighed, the weight of the world on his shoulders. "It appears the Kraang have formed an alliance with your enemy, Shredder."

That was the last thing Leo wanted to hear. "Shredder and the Kraang are working together?"

"That's not all," Kirby admitted. "I fear the Shredder has handed April over to the Kraang."

Donnie's heart began to pound. "Shredder kidnapped April!"

"Dudes, this is getting freakier by the minute!" Mikey said.

"Sensei must have gone after her," Raph realized, putting the pieces of the night together.

"So where is April now?" Donnie asked.

"Shredder said he would hand April over to the Kraang," Kirby told them. "They're taking her to the *Technodrome*."

As if he had summoned it by name, Kirby saw the *Technodrome* appear on the TV in front of him. The local news was reporting the warship's path of destruction throughout the city.

Kirby and the Turtles watched as an intrepid news anchor—with a long, complicated name—stood in front of the terrifying scene: "This is Carlos Chiang O'Brien Gambe here. Pandemonium in the streets as a 'techno-terror-dome' approaches downtown."

Talking over the TV volume, Raph said, "We just escaped that freaky sphere. Now we gotta break into it?"

Kirby nodded. "In a matter of hours, the world we know will be gone. The Kraang want April to help in their conquest of Earth!"

Things were looking bleak for the Turtles: Their sensei was nowhere to be found. Their friend was being held captive. And their planet was in grave danger. They had to save the day—no one else could.

They knew what they had to do.

The Teenage Mutant Ninja Turtles were heading back to the *Technodrome*.

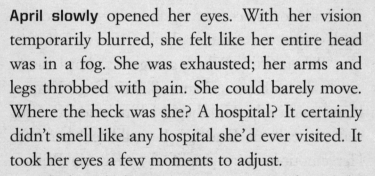

CHAPTER 18

April slowly opened her eyes. With her vision temporarily blurred, she felt like her entire head was in a fog. She was exhausted; her arms and legs throbbed with pain. She could barely move. Where the heck was she? A hospital? It certainly didn't smell like any hospital she'd ever visited. It took her eyes a few moments to adjust.

She heard a booming voice say, "April O'Neil."

Her vision cleared, and now she understood why she couldn't move. There were restraints around her wrists and ankles! She was trapped inside a waking nightmare, held captive inside a sleek control room, surrounded by strange alien devices and video screens. Right in front of her was the biggest Kraang she'd ever seen! Its face stretched from ceiling to floor, set inside a gigantic compartment in the wall.

With a devious smile, it said, "April O'Neil. Kraang has waited a long time."

This wasn't just a giant Kraang, April realized. It had to be a leader, an elder of theirs. A Kraang far more dangerous than she'd ever encountered. She had no choice but to stare directly into the cold, slimy eyes of their ruler . . . Kraang Prime!

"Where am I? What's going on?" April asked.

"Like all Kraang, I am called Kraang," Kraang Prime said coyly. And then it jokingly added, "But you can call me Kraang." It could feel her fear. Her emotions were amplified to Kraang Prime's hyper senses, and it was a sensational feeling for the extra-dimensional kingpin. The time had come to truly frighten her.

"Kraang has need of this planet for Kraang to live on," it said, relishing her reaction to this news.

"Um, that's great, but . . . we're kind of using it," April said. "So you came all this way for nothing? That's a bummer."

"No, Kraang came all this way for you, April O'Neil," it snarled back.

"Aw, you shouldn't have. No, really. You shouldn't have," she said. April stared at Kraang Prime in disbelief. There was no way all of this could be about her. The Kraang needed scientists to help with their evil plot, and she was no scientist. Up until her father's kidnapping, when she was actually applying herself at Roosevelt High School, she was barely passing remedial biology! They had the wrong girl.

Kraang Prime could sense that April didn't know the truth about herself. It decided to enlighten her.

"Your mental energy is uniquely attuned to this universe," Kraang Prime explained. But words could only go so far between the two species. So it decided to psychically "push" the memories into her head, making her remember.

Under Kraang's influence, April experienced her memories in high-speed flashes, one after the other. She recalled the lab monkey she had investigated with Donnie a while ago, and how she had somehow known the mutant's true hidden identity by simply listening to its feelings. Or how, because of some unexplainable instinct, she had been able to excel in her *kunoichi* training with Splinter, despite being a total *ninjutsu* novice. There was something different about her lately. She wasn't feeling like her typical self. At times, she felt like her head might explode because of some unseen force. And now she knew why. She was psychic!

"Once Kraang gains this ability, Kraang will transform your world into a world for Kraang," it proudly announced.

"And how are you going to do that exactly?" April asked hesitantly.

Just then, a mechanism hummed to life with a high-pitched drilling sound. April saw a titanium arm extending toward her. At its very tip was a long, stabbing needle. She struggled, trying to pull away, but it was no use. It was like she was being moved toward it—when she realized she was actually connected to this terrifying machine!

As the machine's arm wound around her, April began to feel dizzy. The last thing she remembered before losing consciousness was opening her mouth to scream.

CHAPTER 19

The fight raged on between Splinter and Shredder. Neither had a clear edge. Both were ninja masters, with lifetimes of experience between them, and as the highest-decorated warriors of their respective *ninjutsu* arts, they were able to match each other's skills step for step. This meant pure deadlock as every kick was met with a kick, every punch with a punch.

Splinter tried to surprise Shredder with a fast strike from his *rokushaku bo,* but Shredder caught the end of the weapon in his blades, pushing his enemy back with a forceful move.

Before Shredder could counter, Splinter pushed a button and released a concealed metal spear tip from the end of his *bo*. Shredder dodged just in time for the glinting tip of the blade to miss his face by a hair.

Now it was the Shredder's turn to attack. He faced his target, then lunged forward with his blades drawn and unleashed a barrage of strikes before finally slicing Splinter's *bo* in half!

Never breaking their stances, the two circled each other, always at the ready for the other's pounce.

"Why must you persist in this insanity?" Splinter asked Shredder.

To Splinter's surprise, Shredder answered, "You took Tang Shen from me!"

"She was never yours!" Splinter defiantly shouted back.

And with the jagged piece of broken *bo* still in his hands, Splinter revealed a secret grappling hook. He swung its chain right as Shredder moved for another attack, taking his legs out and launching him up with one firm pull.

CHAPTER 20

The *Technodrome* brought chaos to the streets of New York City. Throngs of people tried to flee its path, but the war machine's monumental mass made that nearly impossible!

A terrified news reporter and a cameraman were on the scene. "The aliens are here!" the reporter screamed into the camera. "That's right, folks, run for your ever-loving lives, because they're abducting us!"

Suddenly, one of the *Technodrome*'s hydraulic panels opened, releasing a fleet of flying pods!

"That's right, men, women, children—even *pets* aren't safe!" the reporter yelled. A Kraang pod flew down and scooped him up into the ship.

That was the end of his broadcast!

People everywhere were being abducted by the Kraang pods: little old ladies, street performers, math teachers. No one was safe!

In the cockpit of one of the pods, a Kraang-droid pilot repeated its orders from high command. "Kraang must collect human specimens for Kraang."

But some of the droids may have been confused about what the word *human* meant. Some pods were busy abducting alley cats and park pigeons!

Meanwhile, a few blocks away, police officers attempted to maintain law and order during the invasion. "Don't worry, ma'am, the cops are here!" an officer said as he helped a lady to safety. For a brief moment, it seemed he had saved the day— until he was suddenly sucked up into the pod. "Help!" he pleaded. "They're gonna probe me!"

CHAPTER 21

Not far away, the Turtles hid behind the remains of a burnt car, watching the *Technodrome*. They were looking for a way to bust inside and rescue April!

Raph had his game face on. "So, how do we get up there?" he asked.

Leo watched carefully: it seemed the only openings to the *Technodrome* were the docking hatches for the pods. "We gotta get on one of those pods," he deduced out loud.

"But how?" Donnie asked, noticing the ground troop of bots that were heavily armed and watching the street.

"We could create a diversion," Leo answered.

"Excuse me," Raph interrupted. "How many bots are standing guard?"

"Eight."

"I see."

And with that, Raph backed into the shadows.

Mikey was thinking, too. "We dress up like robots . . . sneak in," he suggested.

"Or . . . ," Donnie said, ignoring Mikey, "I could try to override their security codes by—"

"Yaaaa!"

The sound of Raph's signature war cry instantly silenced them.

One by one, Raph slashed and stabbed his way through the rest of the Kraang-droids. Soon there was nothing left but robot parts littering the street, a titanium leg here, a metallic hand there. And for his final trick, Raph leaped off the remains of an exoskeleton, launching himself into the air. He caught a hovering space-pod and pulled it down to earth!

Stunned, Leo could only say, "Or . . . *that* . . . might work. Let's go!"

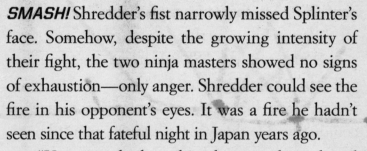

CHAPTER

22

SMASH! Shredder's fist narrowly missed Splinter's face. Somehow, despite the growing intensity of their fight, the two ninja masters showed no signs of exhaustion—only anger. Shredder could see the fire in his opponent's eyes. It was a fire he hadn't seen since that fateful night in Japan years ago.

"You never had anything but your hatred, and if you defeat me, you will have nothing!" Splinter reminded him, and hurled his jagged spear through the air.

With catlike reflexes, Shredder sensed the attack and sprang toward the ceiling, performing a backflip dodge that few warriors in the world could execute. The tip of Splinter's spear flew a fraction of an inch from Shredder's eyes, missing its mark.

"That is where you are wrong," Shredder taunted as he landed on his feet.

Splinter considered this for a moment. He knew Shredder had nothing to live for. That was why he fought with zero hesitation, never fearing death. But that statement . . . He seemed so confident. What did he have up his sleeve?

"You took something from me, so I took something from you," Shredder confessed with an evil grin. "Your daughter!"

A grave look came over Splinter's face. It couldn't be. He thought back to that painful night

The night he'd lost his family forever. Or had he?

Tang Shen's screams echoed through his memories as he thought of the flames his enemy—Oroku Saki—had set to their home. He recalled seeing Oroku Saki running away from the fire, carrying something in his arms. But all these years he'd assumed it was a weapon of some kind, or the torch Saki had used to set the blaze. Never once did he consider it might have been a child. His child. Baby Miwa . . .

Could the daughter of Hamato Yoshi be alive after all these years?

The shock snapped Splinter back to reality. The thought of his only child being raised by Shredder—as his own—was far too much to bear. "No! It can't be!" he yelled.

Seeing Splinter's distraction as the golden opportunity he'd been waiting for, Shredder savagely attacked. The tables had turned!

CHAPTER 23

Hitching a ride on their hijacked space-pod, the Turtles got closer and closer to the *Technodrome*. They could begin to see inside the warship's loading bay. It was a sleek network of mechanical arms that were docking incoming pods and releasing new ones for transport. A hatch leading into the bowels of the ship was just ahead of it. There were no Kraang in sight!

As one of the arms gently guided their space-pod into port, the Turtles saw they were approaching the hydraulic hatch. They prepared for it to open. "Okay, guys, this is it. On three," Leo said. He counted off: "One . . . two . . . three!"

They leaped together just as the ship's hatch

opened. Their plans were suddenly turned upside down . . . literally! Defying all physics, the Turtles found themselves flying upward! They flailed, trying to catch the wall as they flew past, but it was no use. They hit the ceiling at full speed.

"What the heck's going on?!" Raph yelled.

"I think the Kraang forgot to pay their gravity bill!" Mikey replied.

"It appears the Kraang have developed a way to generate anti-gravitons," Donnie informed them as he struggled against the metal ceiling.

"Is there any way for you to generate anti-anti-gravitons?" Leo asked.

Donnie turned to Leo, correcting him. "You mean gravitons?"

"Yes!"

"No."

While Leo and Donnie snapped at each other, Mikey was turning even greener. And for a Turtle, who was already pretty green, this could only mean one thing. "Guys, I'm gonna throw up . . . or down! Or maybe sideways! But one thing's for sure . . . I'm majorly gonna throw!"

Leo knew they needed a way out of the situation, and fast! No one wanted to be covered in a comet of Mikey's vomit! He needed to get their minds off the nausea.

"We still have a job to do," he reminded them. "So let's go."

Using all of his strength, Leo pushed himself off the ceiling and waved his arms to propel his body toward the exit. At first, it was strange. But it soon became easier, like swimming . . . in thin air! The other Turtles saw this and followed his example.

Slowly getting the hang of zero gravity, the Turtles made their way deeper into the *Technodrome,* floating from hiding spot to hiding spot. They eventually came to an area that was filled with Kraang.

There were Kraang-droids floating around, too. And thanks to the zero gravity, they were faster than usual and able to keep a tight patrol on this area of the ship.

Mikey was feeling better now, and having a blast flying around. "Zero-G is bangin'! The Kraang should turn this into a carnival ride!" he shouted.

"I think they're more interested in using it to destroy the earth," Leo told him.

Mikey shrugged. "It could do both."

Suddenly, a piercing wail startled them all into silence. It sounded familiar, like a girl's scream.

"Oh no! It's April!" Donnie exclaimed.

"Can you say that a little louder?" Leo said in a hushed yet angry tone. "I don't think the entire *Technodrome* heard you!"

"Never mind," Raph said, looking around. "They did."

A swarm of Kraang-droids was closing in on them, with their blasters ready.

The Turtles were surrounded!

CHAPTER 24

April O'Neil had a throbbing headache, and in her dizzy state, she could barely keep her eyes open. She could feel the helmet of draining tubes that had been attached to her forehead. If this were an ordinary hospital room, those tubes would have been pumping vitamins or fluids into her body. But here, aboard the *Technodrome,* it was connecting her directly to Kraang Prime, allowing the ruler of the Kraang to siphon her psychic energy at a frightening rate.

A strange yet familiar symbol on Kraang Prime's forehead began to glow. The Kraang ruler laughed diabolically, jarring April back into consciousness for a moment.

"Yes! Yes!" it growled, its power growing.

Squinting, April saw the tubes pump more of her energy, making the head-symbol light shine brighter, almost blinding her.

"It's working!" Kraang Prime proclaimed as its newly acquired power began to charge up the *Technodrome.* All across the ship, lights flickered on. Outside, even the giant eye atop the dome became illuminated.

April wasn't quite sure what was happening, and she was starting to think she might not live long enough to find out.

The Turtles were in the thick of battle with the Kraang-droids when they felt a rumble like an earthquake.

"That can't be good," Leo said, noticing how unstable their alien surroundings had become. It was clear the ship was slowly transforming.

When the walls of the *Technodrome* finally stopped shaking, the Turtles went back to fighting the Kraang-droids. Leo saw more droids coming toward them in sophisticated fly-over attack patterns. But thanks to the zero gravity, the Turtles managed to dodge the Kraang's energy bolts by bouncing between the walls.

And then something clicked in Leo's mind. If they wanted to get the advantage in this midair matchup, they'd have to adapt and use their new-found ability to fly!

As the next wave charged them, Leo drew his trusty *katanas* and flung himself forward in a spinning motion. The zero-G intensified his momentum and sent him zipping through the air like a whirling ninja saw blade. With a tight full-body spiral, Leo cut through a battalion of bots without even breaking a sweat.

The other Turtles were amazed. And inspired! One by one, they drew their weapons and ricocheted themselves off the walls. More Kraang-droids down!

The Ninja Turtles' fight had really taken flight!

CHAPTER 25

Across town, Splinter was also flying through the air, but for a very different reason. Shredder's attacks were becoming more powerful. The armored warrior delivered a fierce *kata*-combo of power punches and speed kicks that sent Splinter sailing backward to the far wall. Shredder was clearly overpowering him, and Splinter began to doubt his chances.

Before Splinter could regain his footing, Shredder brutally kicked him back to the ground. Then he leaned over his opponent's crumpled body. In Splinter's moment of weakness, Shredder no longer saw a mutated rat. He only saw the defeat of his lifelong rival.

He decided to call him by his true name.

"It's over, Hamato," Shredder said, his blades extending from his armor. "Soon you will be no more."

Ignoring his enemy's words, Splinter tried to find whatever strength was still left within him to keep on fighting. He knew deep down that losing now wouldn't just mean sacrificing his own life; it would mean sacrificing the lives of the Turtles, as Shredder would be free to hunt them down with no interference.

Splinter couldn't allow that. He couldn't bear the thought of losing any more children to this monster of a man.

Shredder prepared to deliver what he thought would be the final blow.

Aiming his blades at Splinter's heart, he growled, "And your own daughter will go through her life cursing your name."

That was it. A rage filled Splinter. *Hamato Yoshi may have been defeated by this coward,* he thought, *but Splinter the rat won't be!*

Suddenly, something snared Shredder's wrist, making it impossible to complete his strike. He looked down to see—Splinter's tail! It tightened around his arm and snapped it back like a whip. Using his tail as a snare, Splinter barrel-rolled forward, dragging Shredder helplessly to the ground. The battle was still alive, and so was Master Splinter!

CHAPTER 26

Back inside the *Technodrome,* the Turtles were still walking on air and stomping all the Kraang-droids that crossed their paths! But although it was fun for the Turtles to kick some Kraang butt, there was no reason to celebrate yet. The ship kept deploying more reinforcement droids by the minute, and they were no closer to locating April.

Mikey knew it was time to step up his game.

He readied the throwing chain that rattled out of his *nunchucks* and flung it at a nearby pipe. It wrapped around the pipe with a *CLANG!,* and Mikey used it to swing around an oncoming Kraang-droid.

"Zero-G *booyakashaaaaa*!" Mikey yelled at the top of his lungs. He delivered a midair drop-kick that propelled a Kraang-droid into the wall, where it exploded on contact!

Not one to be outdone—especially by Mikey—Raph was about to plunge his *sais* into a Kraang-droid's face when he pump-faked at the last second and dodged the droid, letting it sail right past him! Raph "swam" through the anti-gravity and caught up to the droid from behind. He leaped onto its back and started riding it like a horse, shouting, "Yeeeehaw! Giddyup!" like a Teenage Mutant Ninja Cowboy! Riding high upon his "trusty steed," Raph cut the bots behind him down to size.

Now it was Donnie's turn. Using the wall, he

pushed off and launched forward like a rocket. Speeding toward the growing number of Kraang heading his way, he opened his *bo* staff and deployed the hidden blade inside. There was no time for the droids to scatter before the blade plunged through every last one of them, skewering their circuitry. They found themselves pinned to the opposite wall like a Kraang-kabob!

The Turtles breathed a sigh of relief. There were no more Kraang in sight!

But their brief moment of victory was cut short by the sound of a booming voice hidden somewhere in the ship. "April O'Neil," the voice roared.

The Turtles floated around, trying to follow the voice to its secret location. Confident that they were floating in the right direction, Raph led them toward a flimsy wall panel. Using all of his strength, he pried it open, revealing a secret passageway. This must be the way to April!

The brilliant light coming from Kraang Prime's forehead now illuminated every inch of the *Technodrome*'s control room. April wasn't moving. She just lay there helplessly in her restraints. The almighty ruler of the Kraang had almost fully drained her of her psychic gift, and in doing so had become one with the warship. Every system on board was powered up to capacity and ready to carry out the final phase of the invasion.

"April O'Neil," Kraang Prime's voice thundered, "your mind belongs to Kraang! Soon, your world will be ours!"

Simply by thinking it, Kraang Prime informed the *Technodrome* of its next command. All at once, radar grids and weapons systems activated in every sector. Outside, the ship pulsed with electric-pink lights coursing through its network, making it glow with a bioluminescent shimmer.

This was the moment Kraang Prime had been waiting for. Earth as humanity knew it was about to change forever.

"Let the planetary mutation begin!" Kraang Prime decreed. It looked over at April, laughing. It didn't care that she was almost unconscious; it wanted her to open her eyes. "Witness the end of your kind!" it snarled at her.

"Not if we can help it!" said a voice from out of nowhere.

It was Leo!

Kraang Prime turned to see the Teenage Mutant Ninja Turtles sailing in to save the day!

"The Turtles!" Kraang Prime hissed angrily. "Kraang will not be stopped by pathetic mutants!"

"At least we're not stupid aliens!" Mikey yelled back at Kraang Prime.

"Raph, quick!" Leo called out.

Raph emerged from behind the Turtles, flying forward like a bullet. As planned, he rocketed toward the alien leader with his *sais* pointed out like a harpoon! *WHAM!* He unleashed a power-strike smack in Kraang Prime's face, hitting the *Technodrome* right where it hurt the most!

Kraang Prime recoiled, screaming in agony from the shocking pain. Because its concentration was shattered, the psychic light of its head-symbol began dimming into nothing.

Meanwhile, the glowing eye atop the dome weakened gradually before shutting down. It was clear something was very wrong with the ship.

The *Technodrome*'s power was nearly gone!

The room began to rumble uncontrollably. Suffering a catastrophic malfunction on all levels, every onboard system failed. The ship went into a severe tailspin. It whirled, sending shock waves through the surrounding area. When it finally came to a stop, the Turtles fell to the floor with a *thud*.

Gravity had been restored!

The Turtles grinned as they stood up. It felt good to be back on their feet and walking around. Donnie rushed over to April and went to work on freeing her from the restraints.

Still dizzy from her traumatic experience, she wasn't sure what was going on at first. But as her mental fog lifted, she recognized Donatello and collapsed into his waiting arms.

"Are you okay?" Donnie asked her.

"You're my hero," she announced groggily.

It was clear that April was momentarily delirious. But Donnie didn't care. He giggled, so happy that the girl of his dreams was alive and well and in his arms. The moment was almost perfect.

Right on cue, Raph ruined it. "Hey, Chuckles!" he said to Donnie. "We gotta get out of here!"

And he was right. The entire room started shaking. The ship was falling apart all around them!

Looking at Kraang Prime, Leo shuddered at the thought of what could have been. The giant Kraang just sat there, motionless. With April's psychic energy gone from its body, and its connective cables to the *Technodrome* severed, Kraang Prime was severely weakened. Leo signaled the Turtles to make their exit.

This time it really was mission accomplished. Time to head for the space-pods and get back home!

The moment Kraang Prime was alone, its eyes shot open. It had survived! With what little power was left in the *Technodrome,* a backup emergency system hummed online. The gears and panels in the room shifted and realigned, making a path for something enormous. But what?

The wall-to-wall compartment that housed the slimy alien suddenly disconnected from the wall, revealing the leader's true form. Titanium arms extended from its sides, followed by robotic legs that lifted it off its base, helping it tower over everything in the room. It stood tall now, looking like the biggest Kraang-droid ever created!

In its terrifying robo-suit, Kraang Prime rumbled toward the outside world, hissing angrily. Target: Turtles!

In Shredder's lair, an epic ninja battle raged. Splinter advanced toward Shredder, forcing him back with surprising strength. This caught Shredder off guard, but just for moment! He countered with a fierce attack, blades out, swinging with deadly force. Splinter dodged these powerful strikes one by one, never losing focus. He quickly yanked a *sai* from his arsenal and broke Shredder's blades in half.

Before Shredder could find his footing,

Splinter grabbed another weapon—a grappling hook—and swung. The hook whirled through the air, spinning, and in one swift move, Splinter tugged it back—pulling off Shredder's mask! His grotesque face was unrecognizable, completely covered in burns and scars.

Unaffected by this disgusting sight, Splinter looked on his enemy's face with zen-like tranquility. All he could see was the fear in Shredder's eyes.

But Splinter wasn't about to walk away. The showdown wasn't over yet. He knew he must destroy Shredder once and for all!

CHAPTER 27

Splinter picked up an ancient *samurai* sword that was lying nearby. Shredder watched, motionless, as he lifted the blade. With one swing, a decades-long feud would finally end. And the memory of an innocent family would finally be avenged! Splinter was about to strike—but a shadowy figure surprised him from behind!

The mysterious warrior attacked with such fury and speed that it was difficult for Splinter to see who he was fighting in the dark. All he could see was another blade. A sword clashing sparks against his.

As Splinter was about to gain the advantage, the unknown sword fighter reversed her move, lunging forward and locking blades with Splinter.

They were at a standstill, staring each other down.

Splinter narrowed his eyes but couldn't believe what he was seeing. It was the familiar face of Tang Shen. Those eyes. But it wasn't his wife. It couldn't be! This was the face of a young girl. A teenager.

"Miwa?" he whispered in disbelief.

It was Karai—Shredder's so-called daughter!

"Father!" she cried as she ran to Shredder's side. She couldn't remember the last time she'd seen him unmasked.

All the rage left Splinter's face. He weakened the grip on his sword, staring at his baby girl. "Miwa?"

"My name is Karai!" she snapped. "Father told me what you did to my mother. And now," she said, training her blade on Splinter, "I'm going to return the favor."

Splinter didn't want to fight anymore. Not when his opponent was his only daughter! But when she charged, he had no choice but to protect himself.

They fought. So skilled was Master Splinter that he was able to duel with Karai without actually harming her. He matched her strike for strike and parried her attacks gracefully, which made her fight even harder. She lunged so angrily, she lost her footing—something that rarely happened to her in battle. She was now completely defenseless. And just as Splinter gained the upper hand in their matchup, with a chance to disable her in one move—he stopped.

Knowing she would never believe his story, Splinter had no option but to retreat. Hopefully, they could meet again someday. Not as enemies, but as family.

Karai watched him drop his weapon and skillfully disappear into the shadows. "Come back! Coward!" she called after Splinter, still blind to the truth about who she really was.

CHAPTER 28

It seemed like the *Technodrome* was about to explode. Pieces of the ceiling were falling in chunks. Sparks rained down. And every Kraang on board was trying to slither its way to safety. The Ninja Turtles raced to the space-pods with April as the floor rumbled beneath their feet. They had to escape this mess quickly or they were going to go down with the ship.

"Leo, I have a question!" Mikey shouted above the chaos.

"Can it wait?" Leo yelled back as huge sections of the *Technodrome* began to burn up behind them.

Mikey thought it over. "Not really!" And then,

glancing behind him, he asked, "Did we beat that Kraang thingie?"

Still running, Leo answered, "Yes, Mikey, we did!"

"Okay," Mikey said. "THEN WHY IS IT FOLLOWING US?!"

They all looked back in unison, and through the falling debris they saw the gigantic figure of Kraang Prime in its mech-suit. And with every mechanical step forward, it was gaining on them!

It lifted its heavy robo-arms and fired a barrage of energy blasts at the Turtles.

"There's nowhere for you to run, mutants!" Kraang Prime hissed.

A stray energy bolt ricocheted, knocking Mikey off his feet. In the commotion, he got separated from his brothers and ended up stranded halfway down a shaft!

Leo looked back in time to see Kraang Prime closing in on Mikey. There was no time to think. He turned and raced back to save him. Sprinting faster and faster under the collapsing ship, he saw

Mikey reach up for help, but Kraang Prime was gaining ground.

"Get away from my brother!" Leo screamed, drawing his *katanas*. Kraang Prime was almost there. But Leo got there first, leaping in at the last second for Mikey's outstretched hand. As Kraang Prime's metal feet landed, Leo swung his blade forward, slicing the energy weapon clean off the droid's body in one forceful swipe!

"Hurry, Mikey!" Leo yelled, pulling his little brother from the shaft. He signaled for Mikey to run away and join the others.

Meanwhile, at the far end of the corridor, Donnie, Raph, and April had reached the loading bay they had sneaked through earlier. There was only one space-pod left. It was their only way out! They jumped inside as the room shook violently all around them. Donnie readied the controls for emergency takeoff just as Mikey boarded. They were good to go—just waiting on their last passenger.

But Leo had something very different to

worry about now. He was left alone, the only thing between his brothers' escape and the evil clutches of Kraang Prime.

"All of you will die here," Kraang Prime threatened.

After one last look at the space-pod behind him, Leo turned and held his blade high toward Kraang Prime. He knew it was only a matter of seconds before the *Technodrome* detonated. The words of Master Splinter echoed in his mind: *With the world at stake, the only thing of importance is that you complete your mission. No matter what you have to sacrifice . . . or who . . .*

He knew what had to be done.

From their pod, Raph watched in horror as Leo charged at Kraang Prime. "Leo!" he shouted.

"No! Get out of here! *Now!*" Leo fearlessly shouted back. He knew his *katanas* would never penetrate Kraang Prime's titanium exoskeleton. But he had to hold it off with something.

And that was when he noticed the chain. Leo picked it up and ran circles with it around

Kraang Prime's robo-limbs. If he couldn't take Kraang Prime on in a ninja fight, he'd at least trap it in one place. Maybe that would give his loved ones the time they needed to escape. Surely it was worth the risk.

From the pod, Mikey yelled, "Dude, you can't do this!"

"I can't hold it back any longer!" Leo pleaded, straining against the power of Kraang Prime's mech-suit.

"Leo!" Raph called out again.

Pulling Raph back in, Donnie closed the pod door, saying, "We've gotta go now!" He pushed a few buttons, activating the controls.

Leo used all of his strength to hold Kraang Prime back. He hoped his brothers and April would make it out alive. But he only managed to buy a few seconds. With a *pop,* Kraang Prime broke free of the chain and ran full speed at the space-pod. Leo fell backward, watching the robo-suited alien lunge for the others.

The pod hummed to life and then blasted off

into the sky, arcing away from Kraang Prime with just inches to spare.

As the pod flew up and away, Raph looked at the scene below from his tiny, round window. He got one last look at the *Technodrome,* and his brother Leo, shrinking away into the distance.

CHAPTER 29

The pod flew out over the Atlantic Ocean and splashed down into the water. After a few moments, the hatch doors opened and Donnie, Raph, Mikey, and April scanned the water's surface.

Donnie said what they were all thinking: "I can't believe it. We made it."

They looked at one another, scared by the thought of what could have become of Leo. The eerie silence was suddenly broken by a strange, high-pitched noise. It sounded a lot like a jet engine multiplied by a million.

They looked up in shock to see—the *Technodrome*! The planet-sized warship was plummeting toward the ocean, plumes of smoke unfurling in its wake!

"Leo! No!" Mikey screamed.

KA-BLAAAAM! The *Technodrome* crashed into the ocean in a tidal wave of flames and water. The impact was so powerful that it nearly capsized the Turtles' pod in an unearthly shock wave. All they could do was watch in terror. The Kraang and everything on board were fish food now. And that included Leo.

It was all too much to bear.

Now it was Mikey's turn to say what they were all thinking. "I can't believe he's gone," he said softly.

They hung their heads in grief.

"Leo," sighed Donnie.

"And I gave him nothing but a hard time," Raph lamented. "If I had it to do over again, I'd definitely be nicer."

"Really?" asked a voice from out of nowhere.

"Really," Raph answered, then realized who he was talking to!

Before he could say another word, they all rushed toward the speaker, looking down over the side of the hatch door. And there, hanging on to the pod and treading water, was Leo! Despite nearly getting crushed by a gigantic Kraang-droid and going through an interdimensional spaceship crash, he had somehow survived! He was a little banged up, but he was all smiles.

"Leo, you dork, you scared the heck out of us!" Raph grumbled.

"You're aliiiiiiiiiiiive!" Mikey cheered.

They excitedly pulled him up into the pod.

Other hover-pods soon splashed down to earth. Their hatch doors opened to reveal more survivors! The humans that the Kraang had abducted were now safe!

There were sighs of relief, high threes, and bro hugs all around. The Teenage Mutant Ninja Turtles had stopped an alien invasion, and they were all alive to see it. This was cause for a major shell-ebration!

CHAPTER 30

Back in the Turtles' lair, the ultimate pizza party was on. Carrying a stack of warm pizza boxes, Mikey made his way to the table and joined everyone for a little victory dance.

"*Who* saved the world?" Mikey chanted.

"We saved the world!" his brothers chanted back.

"I said, *Who* saved the world?"

"We saved the world!"

"I said—"

"Stop asking!" Raph demanded, breaking out of the chant.

Never one to give up on a good cheer, Mikey finished alone with a weak "We saved the world."

On the outskirts of the party, a fully healed

April approached Splinter. Even though the Kraang had put her mind through the wringer, she hadn't forgotten the hurtful things she'd said to her sensei before this whole mess started.

"I wanted to apologize for the way I spoke to you earlier," she told him.

Admiring her conviction, Splinter looked at his *kunoichi* with respect. "No need," he replied gently. "You spoke what was in your heart. I am just relieved that you made it home safely."

April was pleased. She knew he was proud of her, and that was all she really wanted from him. She joined the others for a slice, unaware of the troubled look on Splinter's face.

Splinter moved off to the side, turning his back to the party for a moment. While the others were busy watching Mikey bust a move, Splinter looked at an old photograph—a Yoshi family portrait: Hamato, Tang Shen, and baby Miwa, swaddled in the middle. He couldn't help but study Miwa's face over and over, trying to reconcile the baby in the picture with the teenage assassin he'd seen at Shredder's lair. He didn't know where to begin. He just wanted to be a part of her life.

"What's wrong, Sensei?" he heard Leo ask, just behind him.

Splinter quickly hid the photo. "I learned some things from Shredder," he said.

"Like what?" Leo asked.

"That's for another time, Leonardo," he finally said. "Tonight is for celebration. After all, it is not every day you make the world safe from an alien invasion."

"You got that right!" Mikey said, break-dancing his way into the center of the room.

"Everybody . . . who saved the world?" he cheered again.

"WE SAVED THE WORLD!" everyone joined in.

Meanwhile, deep in the Atlantic Ocean, a school of fish was swimming peacefully along the ocean floor. Suddenly, an unseen force sent a concussion through the water, and the fish flitted away. Strange lights appeared, forming a shape that was round and massive.

The *Technodrome* was badly damaged, but it was back online. It was stranded in the murky depths of the ocean. . . .

But it wouldn't be for long.

FISHFACE

He was once a criminal named Xever, but when he was exposed to mutagen, he became Fishface. This giant fishlike creature has a poisonous bite and robotic legs built by a scientist named Baxter Stockman.

DOGPOUND

While battling the
Turtles, ninja master
Chris Bradford
was doused with
mutagen. He became
a powerful half-man,
half-dog creature
that Michelangelo
nicknamed Dogpound.
He is loyal to his martial
arts master, Shredder.

KRAANG-DROID

The Kraang have built robotic exoskeletons called Kraang-droids that they can control and pilot to fight their enemies.

KRAANG

The Kraang are alien invaders from another dimension with brainlike bodies. They have created a powerful mutagen that they are trying to use to transform and take over the Earth.

FOOT CLAN

Founded as an army of ninja warriors in Japan, the Foot Clan is fanatically loyal to Shredder. They follow their master's every order as he plots to destroy the Turtles.

SHREDDER

Shredder, whose name used to be Oroku Saki,
is a powerful martial arts master and a fierce
underworld boss. Hidden behind armor of
metal blades, he carries a dark secret that